Campaigners

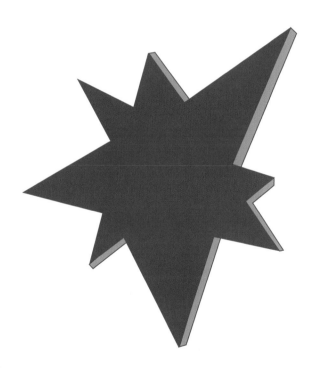

by Paul Thomas

Thameside Press

Distributed in the United States by
Smart Apple Media
1980 Lookout Drive
North Mankato, MN 56003

Text copyright © Paul Thomas

ISBN 1-931983-40-2

Library of Congress Control Number 2002 141370

Printed by Midas, Hong Kong

Editor: Veronica Ross
Series designer: Hayley Cove
Designer: Steve Wilson
Picture researcher: Diana Morris
Consultant: Hazel Mary Martell

Photographic credits
AKG, London: 8(top) Musée Carnavalet; 23(bottom), 27(top). Archive Photos: 21(bottom), 29(top);/Express Newspapers 36(bottom), 40(bottom); 45(bottom). Associated Press/Jackson Daily News/Fred Blackwell: 44(bottom). Bridgeman Art Library: /Giraudon 9 Chateau de Versailles; 10 William Penn House. Brown Brothers: 32(bottom), 33. Camera Press: 26, 31(bottom), 39(bottom). Colorific!/Black Star:/Fred Ward 42; /Charles Moore 43(bottom). Corbis-Bettmann: /UPI 4; 16(top), 19(bottom), 20, 25(top), 30, 31(top), 34, /Reuters 41; /UPI 43(top). Environmental Picture Library: 5(bottom). Mary Evans Picture Library: 6, 11(bottom), 22(top), 22(bottom), 24. Robert Harding Picture Agency:/Gavin Heller 35(bottom). Hulton Getty Collection: 12, 13(top), 23(top), 25(bottom), 29(bottom). Mansell Collection: 8(bottom). Moviestore Collection: 27(bottom). Peter Newark's Pictures: 11(top), 13(bottom), 15, 16(bottom), 17, 19(top), 21(top). North Wind Pictures: 7(top), 7(bottom), 14, 18. Novosti (London): 35(top). Popperfoto: 5(top), 28, 38, 39(top). Redferns:/Ebet Roberts 32(top). Rex Features: 40(top). Frank Spooner/Gamma:/Kaku Kurita 36(bottom); /Ferry-Liaison 37. Topham Picture Source:/AP 44(top).

Words in **bold** appear in the glossary on page 46.

CONTENTS

INTRODUCTION

All over the world, people campaign to change unjust laws or to support a cause that they feel strongly about. In this book, we tell ten fascinating life stories of people who fought for reform and contributed to important changes in world history.

Political campaigners

Thomas Paine was one of the greatest political thinkers of the eighteenth century. He campaigned for freedom and equality and spoke out against slavery. Another important political campaigner was Marcus Garvey. In the 1920s, he encouraged black people to be proud of their African history.

The nineteenth century

One of the most successful campaigns was the fight to end slavery in America. Frederick Douglass and John Brown were leaders of the antislavery movement, which eventually led to the **abolition** of slavery in 1865. In Great Britain at this time, Elizabeth Fry was campaigning for better prison conditions.

Peaceful protest

Twentieth-century campaigners used **civil disobedience** to draw attention to their causes. For example, the Pankhursts chained themselves to buildings to publicize their campaign to win the right for women to vote. In India, Mahatma Gandhi refused to obey British rule, and later in America, African American Rosa Parks sat in a "whites only" bus seat and refused to move.

Martin Luther King, Jr. leads a protest against **segregation** in the United States.

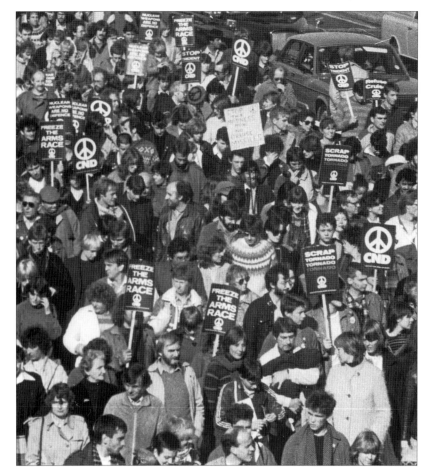

Ban the bomb

Not all campaigns achieve their aims, however. The Campaign for Nuclear Disarmament (CND) has not been successful in its campaign to rid the world of nuclear weapons. But campaigns will continue to happen as long as people feel that a wrong in society can be changed by protest.

A CND march in London, in 1983. The campaigners were protesting against the presence of American **cruise missiles** in England.

Environmental group Greenpeace tries to stop a Norwegian ship from catching and killing whales.

Campaigning on

Some campaigns carry on for many years. Environmental campaigner Jacques Cousteau has been fighting for more than thirty years to protect our planet, its wildlife, and natural resources from pollution.

In South Africa, Nelson Mandela campaigned for over fifty years for the abolition of apartheid. In 1962 he was sentenced to life in prison. Mandela was released when a world-wide protest against apartheid forced the South African government to end its discriminatory policy.

THOMAS PAINE

1737–1809

Thomas Paine, writer and political thinker, campaigned for equality, freedom, and an end to poverty. He was one of the most influential people in eighteenth-century Europe and America.

Thomas Paine was born in 1737, in Norfolk, England. His early life was marked by failures. He trained as a corset-maker and opened his own shop. But the business did poorly, and he was forced to close it down. His next job was as an **excise** officer, tracking down smugglers and collecting taxes on alcohol and tobacco. The wages were poor, and Paine was fired for asking for an increase in pay. His private life was also unhappy. His first wife died, and his second marriage ended in separation.

Adventure-seeker

Paine decided to try his luck in London. While he was there, he met the American politician Benjamin Franklin, who advised him to go to America. Paine had a burning desire for adventure, so he took Franklin's advice. He arrived in America in 1774, and found a job with the *Pennsylvania Magazine*. He became interested in journalism and wrote articles against slavery and in support of women's rights.

Political author and thinker Thomas Paine wanted a world in which everyone would be free and equal.

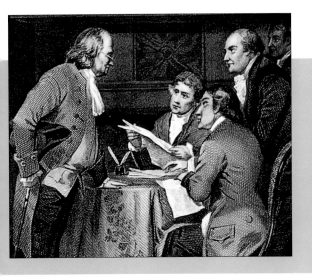

American Independence

The history of the United States began on July 4, 1776, when 13 English **colonies** on the eastern coast of North America declared themselves independent from British rule. The Continental **Congress** drew up the Declaration of Independence, which said that the colonies were free from British control. This painting shows colonists drafting the declaration.

Best-seller

In 1775 feelings against Great Britain ran high. Paine played an active role. In his book *Common Sense*, which was published in 1776, Paine said that Americans should cut all links with Great Britain and demand complete independence. The book became a best-seller, and more than 500,000 copies were sold in just a few months. Many Americans were not sure that breaking away from Great Britain was the right thing to do, but *Common Sense* helped to persuade them that it was.

The Crisis papers

Between 1776 and 1783, Paine wrote the 16 Crisis papers. During the long, cold winter of 1776–1777, these pamphlets were handed out to the American troops to encourage them to continue the fight for freedom. The first pamphlet, called *The American Crisis*, opened with the words, "These are the times that try men's souls."

Rebel American forces fighting British soldiers at the Battle of the Brandywine, near Philadelphia, during the American Revolution.

The French Revolution

In 1789 riots broke out in Paris, France. French citizens were tired of paying high taxes to support the lavish lifestyle of King Louis XVI and his wife, Marie Antoinette. In July 1789 angry crowds stormed the Bastille, an ancient prison and symbol of royal power. They demanded an end to the monarchy and the establishment of a French **republic**. The king and queen, and thousands of nobles were executed in a violent reaction to the old system of rule.

Poverty-stricken

Despite the success of his book, Paine was penniless after the war. He made no money on his books and papers because he wanted them to be sold as cheaply as possible so that everyone would be able to buy them. George Washington, leader of the American Army and first president of the United States, realized the important role that Thomas Paine had played in the American Revolution. He helped him find somewhere to live and gave him a **pension**.

The Rights of Man

But Tom Paine was not a man to settle into early retirement. In 1787 he returned to England, where he wrote *The Rights of Man* (1791–1792) in support of the French Revolution. Paine believed that monarchies should be abolished in favor of republics. In the same book, he called for an end to poverty, **illiteracy**, and unemployment. He also described his ideas for pensions for elderly people, education for children, and relief for the poor.

Found guilty

These ideas were thought to be **radical** and dangerous. The book was banned in England, and the publisher was sent to prison. Orders went out for Paine's arrest, but he escaped to France. He was tried in his absence, was found guilty, and was declared an outlaw.

An eighteenth-century political cartoon passing judgment on Tom Paine. Many people thought he was crazy and dangerous.

In August 1792, French revolutionaries
stormed the Tuileries, where Louis XVI
was living, and imprisoned the royal family.

Imprisoned in France

Paine stayed in France and was elected a
member of the National Convention, which
was the new revolutionary parliament.
He joined in the call for the abolition of
the French monarchy, but he spoke out
against the violence and the large number
of executions. In 1793 Paine was thrown
into prison because he tried to stop the
revolutionaries from executing Louis XVI.

During this time, Thomas Paine wrote
his last great work, *The Age of Reason*. In
this book he attacked religion, which he
said was just superstition. Paine was
released from prison after about a year.
He stayed in France after his release and
rejoined the National Convention.

Changing times

In 1802 Paine returned to America, but
times had changed, and the American
people had forgotten his contribution to
the American Revolution. They were
angry about his attacks on Christianity
in *The Age of Reason*, and for the last few
years of his life, Tom Paine was forgotten
and ignored. He died on June 8, 1809.

Radical ideas

Thomas Paine spent his life campaigning
for freedom and basic human rights. Many
of his ideas, such as his plans for popular
education, relief for the poor, and pensions,
were ahead of their time and considered
too radical to be taken seriously. But his
influence was far-reaching. During the
twentieth century, Paine has been rightly
recognized as one of the greatest political
campaigners in history.

ELIZABETH FRY

1780–1845

English prison reformer Elizabeth Fry spent most of her life campaigning to improve conditions in prisons throughout Europe.

In the seventeenth and eighteenth centuries, conditions in English prisons were appalling. The cells were filthy and overcrowded, with men and women packed in together. Many prisoners died of diseases, such as cholera and typhus, that they caught while in prison.

People were imprisoned for committing even minor crimes, such as stealing a loaf of bread. Other prisoners were people who were mentally ill. They should not have been in prison at all, but there was nowhere else for them to go.

Schoolteacher

Elizabeth Gurney was born in Norwich, England, in 1780. She was the daughter of a wealthy Quaker banker, and she grew up in a large, happy family. When she was 17, Elizabeth began visiting the poor people in her village. She soon became aware of the differences between her life and the lives of the villagers. She tried to think of ways to help, and she set up a school so that she could teach the local children to read and write. In 1800 she married Joseph Fry, a Quaker and local merchant.

Elizabeth Fry, one of the most important campaigners for prison reform in Europe.

Shocking conditions

In 1813 Stephen Grellet, an American friend of Elizabeth's and a fellow Quaker, visited Newgate Prison, in London. He was shocked by what he saw. Men, women, and children shared the same cells, and all the prisoners had lice and fleas. The children were thin and underfed and ran around half-naked. One cell housed 300 women. Many of them were drunk, and they were fighting and swearing.

Improving the prisons

Grellet described what he had seen to Elizabeth. She could not believe what he told her, so she decided to visit Newgate to see for herself. The prison was exactly as Grellet had described it. Elizabeth was so horrified that she decided she must try to help the prisoners and improve conditions in the prison.

Elizabeth Fry visiting female prisoners in Newgate Prison. Many of the women were so violent that the prison governor refused to walk among them.

Quakers

The real name for the Quakers is The Society of Friends. The society was formed in the seventeenth century and later spread to Africa, Asia, and America. Quakers do not have clergypersons because they believe that everyone has a special relationship with God. They hold meetings, but they do not recite prayers or sing hymns. The Society of Friends are **pacifists** and believe that education is very important. They also believe in equality for everyone.

Better conditions

Fry complained to the prison authorities and told them that they should make sure the food was nutritious, especially for the children in prison.

She collected bundles of old clothes from her friends and family and gave the women sewing materials and cloth so that they could mend their old clothes and make new ones for themselves and their children. The women were also allowed to make patchwork quilts, which they could sell to make a little money.

Fry set up a school in Newgate Prison and taught the prisoners how to read and write. At first the prison authorities opposed her work, thinking that the prisoners would not appreciate it. But Fry was able to show them that the prisoners behaved better when they were treated well.

New laws

As a result of Fry's campaign, the British Parliament introduced laws to improve the conditions in all prisons. Women wardens were employed to look after women prisoners, men and women had separate cells, and all jails were inspected regularly.

Convict ships

British prisons were so overcrowded that many prisoners were sent to **penal colonies** in Australia. The journey by ship took several weeks, and the conditions onboard were terrible because so many prisoners were packed into a small area. Fry visited 106 convict ships before they left for Australia and forced the authorities to allow enough space for the prisoners to move around. She succeeded in transforming the convicts' voyage.

Teaching prisoners to read the Bible in Newgate Prison, in 1814.

Prisoners caged like animals onboard a convict ship bound for Botany Bay, Australia.

International fame

Fry's fame as a campaigner and prison reformer spread to other countries. Between 1818 and 1843, she visited prisons in Ireland, France, Belgium, the Netherlands, Prussia, and Denmark. Wherever she went, people asked her how they could improve their prisons.

Mourned by thousands

Ill health finally forced Fry to stop traveling. She remained disabled by illness for the last few years of her life and died in 1845. Thousands of people gathered at her funeral to mourn her death.

Prisons

Today the most common form of punishment for people who commit serious crimes is imprisonment. But a prison sentence for a criminal offense is quite a modern development. Until the eighteenth century, most criminals were likely to be whipped, branded with a hot iron, or even executed. Prisons were used mainly for political prisoners who were held because of their beliefs.

JOHN BROWN

1800–1859

John Brown is an unusual figure in American history. He was a white man who fought for the freedom of black slaves in the United States.

John Brown was born in Connecticut, in 1800, but his family moved to Ohio when he was five years old. John's father owned a leather **tannery**. When John left school, he went to work for his father and then set up a business on his own.

Financial hardships

John Brown was a poor businessman, and he struggled to make enough money to support his wife and children. He invested money in land, only to lose most of it when prices dropped. Then he started a sheep farm, but that went bankrupt in 1842. Most of the time, his family suffered terrible financial hardships.

The search for a better life

Brown and his family moved several times in search of a better life. In 1849 they settled in a black community at North Elba, New York, on land donated by an antislavery supporter. Despite his own hardships, Brown could see that many black people were far worse off.

Militant antislavery campaigner John Brown helped to bring about the abolition of slavery in the United States.

Slave state

At this time, many Africans living in the United States were still slaves. Some of the northern states had abolished slavery, and former slaves had found work on building sites or in factories. But their wages were so low that they could not afford to feed their families, and the conditions they lived in were little better than those of slavery.

In 1855 Brown moved to Kansas, where slavery was still legal. He became involved in the antislavery movement and joined in peaceful protests calling for freedom for all black men and women.

Violent times

But when an antislavery supporter was murdered and the culprit allowed to go free, Brown decided that peaceful protests were a waste of time. He soon became convinced that the only way to fight the injustice of slavery was with violence.

Pottawatomie Creek

One night in May 1856, John Brown and four of his sons rode into Pottawatomie Creek, in Kansas, to raid a proslavery settlement. Five people were murdered. The massacre had the effect Brown had hoped it would. More and more people joined the antislavery movement, and fighting broke out between antislavery and proslavery forces. Finally, the American government agreed to abolish slavery in Kansas.

Slave labor

About six million Africans were transported to America during the eighteenth century. They were sold at auctions and taken to work on the plantations, where they were used as slave labor to cultivate crops of tobacco, cotton, and sugarcane. During the nineteenth century, many people began to campaign against slavery. Former slaves were encouraged to tell their stories and to describe the beatings and cruel treatment they had experienced at the hands of their owners. This early photograph, taken in about 1860, shows a family of slaves working in the fields.

Harpers Ferry

Brown turned his attention to the abolition of slavery in other southern states. In 1859, with a band of armed supporters, Brown captured a government **armory** at Harpers Ferry, in western Virginia. Harpers Ferry was the entrance to the Great Black Way. This was the route slaves used to escape from the slavery of the southern states to freedom in the north.

Brown hoped that news of his attack would spread, and that slaves in the area would join him. His plan was to give them guns from the armory and start a slave revolt. About three of the four million slaves in the United States lived in this area, and Brown thought that such a large number would make a revolt unstoppable.

John Brown preparing to fight, as United States marines break down the door of the armory at Harpers Ferry.

Uprising and capture

But the uprising did not go according to plan. Government troops surrounded the armory and stopped the rebels from passing the weapons out to their supporters.

After two days, United States marines stormed the building. The government wanted to capture the rebels, dead or alive. Ten men were killed, including two of Brown's sons, and John Brown and the rest of the group were captured.

Day of execution

The rebels were tried for murder, slave **insurrection**, and **treason** against the state. They were sentenced to death. On December 2, 1859, Brown kissed his wife and family good-bye and visited his companions for the last time. Then he was led out to be hanged.

More than 3,000 soldiers formed a 16-mile (25-km) circle around the scaffold to keep back Brown's supporters and to prevent any last-minute attempts to rescue him.

The Last Moments of John Brown, by Thomas Hovenden (1884). Brown became a hero after his death. The song "John Brown's Body" was a marching song for Union troops during the Civil War.

Nat Turner

One of the most famous revolts against slavery was led by Nat Turner, a black slave. Turner believed that through violence he would win freedom for all slaves. In August 1831, Turner and six other slaves killed their owner. Over the next two months, 56 white people were murdered. Turner was captured in October 1831, and executed. John Brown was influenced by this revolt, which changed the idea that slaves were content in their chains.

The abolition of slavery

John Brown met his death calmly and bravely. For many Americans he was a **martyr** who had sacrificed his life in the fight for freedom. His actions helped to spread the call for the abolition of slavery throughout the United States. Slavery was finally abolished in 1865.

FREDERICK DOUGLASS

1817–1895

Frederick Douglass, former slave and antislavery campaigner, became one of the most important human rights leaders of the nineteenth century.

Frederick Bailey was born into slavery in Maryland, in 1817. He was separated from his mother when he was a baby and sent to live with his grandmother. When he was seven or eight, he was sold to Hugh Auld, a slaveowner from Baltimore.

This move was an important turning-point in Frederick's life. He was sent to work as a servant in the plantation house, where he made friends with Auld's wife, Sophie. She ignored the state law, which said that slaves must not be educated, and taught Frederick to read. Many years later, Frederick said that learning to read was his "pathway from slavery to freedom."

Unfit for slavery

Hugh Auld was angry when he found out that Frederick could read. He told his wife that black people should not be educated because it made them unfit for slavery and gave them ideas about escaping. As punishment, Auld sent Frederick to work for Edward Covey, a violent man who ruthlessly beat his slaves.

Frederick Douglass was the first African American to hold high office in the United States government.

Slave hunters and their dogs chasing an escaped slave.

Learning to write

But Frederick stood up to Covey's brutal treatment. One day he told Covey that if he hit him once more, he would fight him until one of them was killed. Covey realized that he would never break Frederick's spirit, so he sent him back to Hugh Auld's plantation in Baltimore.

Auld died shortly after Frederick's return, and Frederick was sent away to learn ship **caulking**. He taught himself to write by tracing the letters on the **prows** of the ships.

Escape from slavery

Frederick made his first attempt to escape from slavery when he was 16, but his plans were discovered before he could get away. Five years later, disguised as a free black seaman, Frederick caught a train to New York City. He changed his last name to Douglass to hide his real identity. He had escaped, but he was not a free man.

Slave autobiographies

Between 1820 and 1860, many books were written by slaves about their lives. They described the slaves' experiences on the plantations, their escape to freedom, and their fight to abolish slavery. The most popular books were those written by Frederick Douglass, Moses Roper, and Solomon Northup. Each book sold thousands of copies and was translated into many languages.

NARRATIVE

OF THE

LIFE

OF

FREDERICK DOUGLASS,

AN

AMERICAN SLAVE.

WRITTEN BY HIMSELF.

BOSTON:
PUBLISHED AT THE ANTI-SLAVERY OFFICE.
No. 25 Cornhill
1845.

Publishing a best-seller

Douglass moved to Massachusetts, where he became involved in the campaign to abolish slavery. In 1841 he told his life story at an antislavery meeting. Douglass spoke so well many people could not believe that he had been a slave. His lectures became very popular, and he was encouraged to write the story of his life. It was published in 1845, as *Narrative of the Life of Frederick Douglass, An American Slave.* The book became a best-seller.

Lecture tour

Douglass left the United States to escape the slave hunters, and he went on a lecture tour of Great Britain and Ireland. During the tour, he made many friends, and they raised the money for him to buy his freedom.

Abraham Lincoln

During his campaign to be elected president of the United States in 1860, Abraham Lincoln spoke out against slavery. He believed that slavery was evil and should be abolished. But the economy in the southern states relied heavily on the slaves who worked on the plantations where crops of sugarcane and cotton were grown. Many southerners were against Lincoln's policy to abolish slavery, and in 1865, he was shot and killed by a fanatical supporter of the southern states.

The *North Star*

When he returned to the United States, Douglass started an antislavery newspaper, called the *North Star,* to put forward his views. He was a brilliant journalist and wrote many articles about the evils of slavery.

Douglass also campaigned for the **civil rights** of free black people. They had been released from slavery, but many found it difficult to find work because they were **discriminated** against.

A nineteenth-century etching showing Frederick Douglass, writer and statesman, at work in his office in Washington, D.C.

Lincoln's wartime consultant

During the war, President Lincoln asked Frederick to work with him as a consultant. Douglass said that former slaves should be armed and allowed to fight. He helped to raise two **regiments** of black soldiers, and his three sons joined the army.

Ambassador to Haiti

Slavery was finally abolished in 1865. After the war, Douglass held several positions in the American government. In 1889 he became the American ambassador to Haiti. He was the first black person to have such an important job.

Douglass's powerful speeches and his work in the government helped to end slavery and improve the lives of black people in the United States. In 1895, at the age of 78, Douglass died of a heart attack in Washington, D.C.

War breaks out

In 1861 the Civil War broke out. The war split the United States in two, as north and south fought over the issue of slavery. In the northern states of America, most black people were free, but in the southern states, black people were still slaves. The war began when some of the southern states broke away from the United States and formed the Confederacy. At first the Confederates seemed to be winning, but the northern army fought back and defeated the Confederacy in 1865.

A photograph of the 107th U.S. infantry, taken during the Civil War. It was America's first black regiment.

THE PANKHURSTS

EMMELINE PANKHURST 1858–1928

CHRISTABEL PANKHURST 1880–1958

Emmeline and Christabel Pankhurst were the leaders of the **women's suffrage** movement that campaigned to win the vote for women in Great Britain.

Toward the end of the nineteenth century, there was a growing interest in women's rights, and women all over the world began to campaign for the right to vote. Women in New Zealand won the vote in 1893, and Australia followed in 1902. But in Great Britain, most men thought that women should not be concerned with politics.

At this time, British women had very few rights. It was difficult for them to start a profession, attend a university, or become involved in politics.

The Pankhurst family

In Great Britain, the Pankhurst family, led by Emmeline Pankhurst and her daughters, Christabel, Sylvia, and Adele, began the fight for the vote.

Emmeline was born in Manchester, England, in 1858. She studied in Paris, France, and returned to England to marry Richard Pankhurst, a lawyer. In 1889 Emmeline helped set up the Women's Franchise League. In 1894 this won the right for married women to vote in local elections.

Militant campaigners for women's suffrage Emmeline Pankhurst (top) and her daughter Christabel.

"Votes for women!"

In 1903 Emmeline set up the Women's Social and Political Union (WSPU) to campaign for women's suffrage. Before long the women were called "suffragettes." The union's slogan was "Deeds not Words," and from the very beginning, the Pankhursts organized marches and demonstrations. They burst into political meetings waving banners and shouting, "Votes for women!"

A militant campaign

But these protests did not achieve very much. Christabel convinced her mother that the suffragettes should become more militant. So the women launched a new campaign and went to great lengths to have their cause taken seriously.

Emmeline Pankhurst being carried away by police after a suffragette attack on Buckingham Palace, in May 1914.

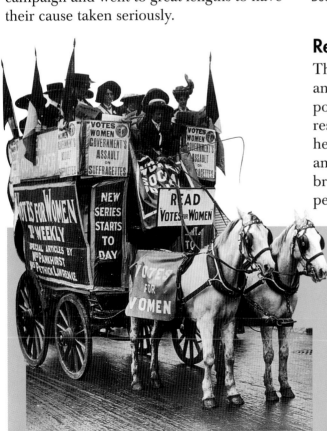

Resisting arrest

They chained themselves to lampposts and smashed store windows, and when the police were called to the scene, the women resisted arrest. In 1913 Emily Davison threw herself under the king's horse at the Derby, and was killed. Incidents such as these brought the suffragettes publicity and made people aware of their campaign.

The women's movement

During the twentieth century, women's organizations continued to campaign for equal pay, education, and job opportunities. Laws have been passed in Europe and in the United States that ban sex discrimination in the workplace. But there are still very few women in high-paying jobs, and throughout the world women continue to earn less than their male colleagues for doing the same work.

A dramatic suffragette poster from the early 1900s, criticizing the government's policy of force-feeding women in prison.

Government action

The women in prison carried on their protest by going on a hunger strike. But the British government took firm action against them, and the women were force-fed. People were outraged when they learned how the suffragettes were treated.

Cat and mouse

In 1913 the Prisoners (Temporary Discharge for Ill Health) Act was passed. It was nicknamed the "Cat and Mouse Act." Under this act, women hunger strikers were released from prison when they became ill, but arrested again as soon as they were better. This happened to Emmeline Pankhurst 12 times. On one occasion she went to a suffragette meeting on a stretcher.

War breaks out

Such determination brought the suffragette movement so much support that it seemed women would soon get the vote. But in 1914 World War I broke out. The British government released all the suffragettes who were still in prison, and the Pankhursts called off the campaign. Emmeline and Christabel knew that the suffragettes would lose a lot of support if they continued to challenge the government while the country was at war. Instead, they advised women to support the war effort and go to work for their country.

World War I (1914–1918)

In June 1914 Archduke Ferdinand, heir to the Austrian throne, was murdered by a Serbian **nationalist**. This event triggered the start of World War I. Within weeks, Austria had declared war on Serbia, and Europe was split into two camps. Russia went to the aid of the Serbs, along with its allies, Great Britain and France, and Germany declared war on Russia. Other European powers soon allied with one side or the other. Millions of men went to fight, and more than ten million people were killed.

Women at war

The suffragettes took jobs in factories, making weapons and ammunition, and helped run public services, such as the postal service. The war was the first time that many women had worked, and they proved that they could do the jobs as well as, if not better than, men. When the war ended in 1918, public support was behind the suffragette movement, and women over the age of 30 were given the vote. In 1928 the age was lowered to 21, which finally put women on an equal footing with men.

Freedom fighters

The Pankhursts made a huge contribution to the freedom of women by fighting for the right to vote. After the war, Emmeline lectured on child welfare. Christabel settled in the United States, and wrote her life story, *Unshackled: The Story of How We Won the Vote*.

A woman working in a **munitions** factory during World War I.

MAHATMA GANDHI

1869–1948

Political and religious leader Mahatma Gandhi inspired millions of Indians to join him in his campaign to win independence for India.

In the 1850s, about two-thirds of India was ruled by Great Britain. The Raj (the British government in India) made all the decisions about how India should be run. But toward the end of the nineteenth century, a new nationalist movement began to take hold in India. Members of the movement believed that Indians should be in charge of their own country and that it was time for the British to go. In 1885 the Indian National Congress campaigned for small changes in the government. When these changes were refused, they started to campaign for home rule.

Young lawyer

Mohandas Karamchand Gandhi was born in 1869, in Porbandar, in western India. His father and grandfather were local officials in the Raj. Gandhi was married when he was just 14. In 1887 he left his wife and son in India, and went to London to study law. He returned to India in 1891 and tried to make a living as a lawyer. But the legal profession was very overcrowded, and it was difficult for him to find a job.

Gandhi was determined to free India from British rule. His nonviolent protests persuaded Indians to join his fight for freedom.

Racial discrimination

After two years, Gandhi accepted a job with an Indian law firm in South Africa. Many Asian people lived there. They had **emigrated** to find jobs, but they were disliked by the white South Africans. Soon after Gandhi's arrival in South Africa, he suffered **racial harassment** because he was not white. He was thrown off a train and was refused entry to hotels.

Gandhi protested the way Asians were treated and began a campaign against racial discrimination. He led peaceful protests and refused to use violence. He said, "I am prepared to die, but I am not prepared to kill." He was arrested and thrown into prison, but he never hit back at his enemies.

A simple life

When Gandhi returned to India in 1915, the Indian National Congress had become more militant. They wanted the British to leave India. They asked Gandhi to become their leader, but he refused. He wanted to live a simple life on his farm, where he grew his own food and spun yarn to make clothes.

Gandhi outside his law office, in South Africa.

Political leader

Gandhi did not want to become involved in politics, but he changed his mind in 1919. This was the year of the Amritsar Massacre, when hundreds of Indians were killed by the British Army.

The Amritsar Massacre

In April 1919 a crowd of unarmed Indians in Amritsar, northern India, protested against British rule. General Dyer, a British officer, thought the protesters were threatening and ordered his soldiers to open fire. Nearly 400 people were killed. The massacre made the cause of Indian independence more popular in India and throughout the world. This picture is from the film *Gandhi*, released in 1982.

Boycotting the British

Gandhi decided that he must take direct action. He agreed to become the leader of the Indian National Congress, and in 1920 he launched a policy of **noncooperation** with the British. He encouraged Indians to **boycott** British goods. Many Indians gave up their jobs in the local government and refused to obey British authorities. They sat and blocked the streets, refusing to move, even when they were beaten by the police.

Hunger strike

Gandhi was arrested several times, and each time, he went on a hunger strike as part of his campaign of civil disobedience. The British authorities found it hard to deal with him because he was never angry or violent.

The ruined remains of a house owned by a rich Hindu banker that was destroyed by Muslims.

The Salt March

The Salt March was the most spectacular campaign against British rule in India. In 1930 Gandhi led thousands of people on a 200-mile (320-km) walk to the coast, where he took salt from seawater. This was in direct protest against the British government tax on salt. Everyone in India was forced to buy salt from the state, even though they could make it very cheaply themselves.

Religious problems

In 1922 Gandhi was imprisoned for two years. When he was released, he decided to withdraw from politics. The continuous fighting between India's two main religious groups, the Muslims and the Hindus, was a major problem for Gandhi. Followers of both religions found it impossible to live peacefully together, and this made it very difficult to unite India in its struggle for independence.

Violent explosion

The religious conflict was still a problem. Gandhi tried to find a solution, but the differences between the Hindus and the Muslims were too great. In 1947 India was **partitioned**, and Pakistan was created as a separate Muslim state. Millions of people were forced to leave their homes, and there was an explosion of violence between the Hindus and Muslims. Millions were killed.

Gandhi's funeral procession passes through Bombay. His ashes were scattered in fifty rivers in India and Pakistan.

Independence for India

Gandhi reentered politics in 1930, launching a second campaign of noncooperation. Finally, the British agreed to begin talks on India's self-government, and in 1947 India became independent.

Great soul

Gandhi was against the partition, and his disappointment that India had been divided made the Hindus very angry. In January 1948, Gandhi was **assassinated** at a peace rally in New Delhi, by a Hindu **extremist**. Although he died violently, Gandhi's message was that peaceful protests always win in the end. He is known all over the world as *Mahatma*, which means "great soul."

MARCUS GARVEY

1887–1940

Jamaican campaigner Marcus Garvey organized one of the first black nationalist movements to fight for the rights of black people. He is remembered as a national hero in Jamaica.

During the seventeenth and eighteenth centuries, millions of Africans were captured and transported to America, where they were sold into slavery. When slavery was abolished in 1865, many Africans dreamed of returning to their homelands, where they could live in freedom. But by 1900, most of Africa was governed by European powers, such as Great Britain, France, and Germany. Only Liberia and Ethiopia remained independent.

Strike leader

Marcus Garvey was born on the Caribbean island of Jamaica, in 1887. When he was 14, he left school to become a printer's apprentice. A few years later, he took a job with a printing firm in the capital, Kingston, where he led a strike for higher wages and better working conditions. After the strike Garvey lost his job. Finding another one was difficult because employers regarded him as a troublemaker. So Garvey decided to leave Jamaica for Central America.

Marcus Garvey at the height of his power in 1920. His followers called him "Black Moses."

Booker T. Washington

Booker T. Washington was born into slavery in America, in 1856. When he was a young man, slavery was abolished, and he was able to go to college, where he trained to become a teacher. Washington believed that education was more important than anything else. With the help of his students, he built his own college for black students at Tuskegee, Alabama. Washington's autobiography, *Up from Slavery*, has been a great influence on many black leaders in the twentieth century.

African culture

In 1912 Garvey traveled to London, where he read *Up from Slavery*, the autobiography of Booker T. Washington. The book captured Garvey's imagination. He became interested in African history and in the struggle of African people to escape from slavery.

Back to Africa

Garvey believed that Africans should be proud of their traditions. In London, he met people who talked about African customs and beliefs, and traditions of art and music. He began to dream about creating a black-governed nation in Africa.

In 1914 Garvey returned to Jamaica, where he set up the Universal Negro Improvement Association (UNIA). The organization wanted to improve the living standards of black people everywhere and to encourage black people to return to their native lands, where they would build a black nation. This movement was called "Back to Africa."

UNIA officials with Marcus Garvey in the center of the group.

A growing organization

Garvey traveled to the United States to win support for his organization. He was a powerful speaker, and in a short time he gained a large following. He told black people that they could do great things if they believed in themselves and worked together. Branches of the UNIA were set up all over America and Africa.

With the money from his supporters, Garvey set up grocery stores, restaurants, a newspaper, and a fleet of steamships that would return people to Africa.

Street parade

At the peak of his power, Marcus Garvey had about one million followers. In 1920 he headed an international conference in New York City, with representatives from 25 countries. The conference ended with a parade through the streets of Harlem.

Shattered dreams

But some of Garvey's business methods came under suspicion and, in 1923, he was arrested for **fraud**. He was found guilty and imprisoned for two years. In 1927 he was **deported** to Jamaica.

Garvey was a deeply disappointed man. The UNIA had been banned in African countries, and his plans for a black-run nation in Africa lay in ruins. In 1935 he returned to London, where he tried to start a new movement, but it failed. Marcus Garvey died in poverty, in 1940.

Marcus Garvey, handcuffed to a police officer, is led away after his arrest for fraud.

Rastafarians

Marcus Garvey was a major force behind the Rastafarian movement, which began in Jamaica, in the 1930s. Rastafarians believed that Haile Selassie, or Ras Tafari, Emperor of Ethiopia, was the living God. The movement is named after him. For many Africans, Ethiopia is the birthplace of African nationalism. Rastafarians have their own musical style called reggae. Bob Marley, left, was a Rastafarian. He became one of the most famous reggae musicians in the world.

Hope for the future

Since his death, Marcus Garvey has become one of the best-known black leaders of the twentieth century. He brought pride, self-respect, and hope for the future to black people all over the world, by teaching them about their African heritage. In 1962, when Jamaica became independent, Marcus Garvey was named as one of the island's national heroes. His tomb, which stands in a park in Kingston, has become a national **shrine**.

African independence

During Garvey's lifetime, his plans for an independent African state seemed far-fetched. Many governments thought that Garvey was a troublemaker, and he was accused of giving black people false hope. But his ideas inspired many Africans to fight for equality, and today most African countries have become independent.

In 1920 UNIA members elected Marcus Garvey provisional president of Africa. More than 50,000 people took part in a parade through the streets of Harlem to celebrate the event.

JACQUES COUSTEAU

Born 1910

Although he is best known as an undersea explorer, Jacques Cousteau has spent much of his life campaigning on behalf of the environment and the world's wildlife.

Jacques-Yves Cousteau was born in France, in 1910. When he was 20, he entered the French Naval Academy. Three years later, Cousteau joined the French Navy as a second lieutenant and was stationed at Toulon, on the Mediterranean coast.

The aqualung

Over the next few years, Cousteau became interested in underwater diving. With another Frenchman, Émile Gagnan, he designed the first aqualung. This invention consisted of air cylinders containing compressed air, and a mouthpiece that fed air to a diver. Divers could descend to depths of 200 feet (60 m) without having to wear heavy protective suits, and they were able to spend long periods of time underwater.

War hero

When World War II (1939–1945) began, Cousteau served with the **French Resistance**. He was a courageous fighter, and at the end of the war, he was awarded the Croix de Guerre. This is one of the highest honors France can give its people.

Jacques Cousteau celebrating his 75th birthday on board his ship, *Calypso*.

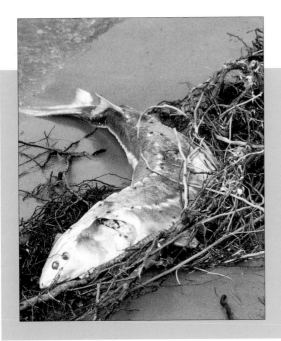

Pollution

Over the years people have polluted the Earth, either accidentally or on purpose. Tropical rain forests have been cut down, oil tankers have spilled oil, and **toxic waste** has been dumped into rivers and seas, killing fish and other wildlife. These are just some of the environmental disasters that are happening today.

Environmental groups, such as Friends of the Earth and Greenpeace, campaign to make the public more aware of this destruction. They hope that by gaining public support they can make our planet cleaner and safer for everyone.

Underwater films

In 1946 Cousteau founded the Undersea Research Group, which was part of the French Navy. He worked on the dangerous job of clearing unexploded mines from the sea.

He also began to make scientific films underwater. Cousteau proved to be a skilled underwater photographer and, in 1957, his film *The Golden Fish* won an Academy Award for the best short film.

Exploring the oceans

During the 1950s, Cousteau went on many explorations on behalf of the National Geographic Society in his specially built **oceanographic** research ship, *Calypso*. These included an expedition to the Red Sea in 1951, and a four-year survey of the world's oceans that began in 1952.

A deep-sea diver using an aqualung.

Nuclear power

Nuclear power plants, like the one in Japan shown here, provide us with electricity but also produce waste that is extremely **radioactive**. The waste matter is held in heavy lead or concrete **shields** to keep it from poisoning people or the environment.

Environmental campaigners have often warned that the risk of a nuclear accident is too great to continue producing energy this way. On April 24, 1986, they were nearly proved right when a **reactor** at the Chernobyl nuclear power plant in the Ukraine, exploded.

The world beneath the oceans

Cousteau continued to make films, and his television program, "The Undersea World of Jacques Cousteau," ran for ten years all over the world. Through this program, Cousteau was able to show people the wonderful creatures that live in the ocean.

Nuclear waste

In 1960 Cousteau became involved in a campaign to stop the planned dumping of nuclear waste in the Mediterranean Sea. Governments listened to him because they knew he cared about the environment, and the plans to dump the waste were dropped.

Cousteau also protested against nuclear energy and nuclear weapons. He believed that nuclear energy was dangerous and worried there would be an environmental tragedy if countries continued to dump their nuclear waste in the oceans.

Jacques Cousteau preparing to descend 330 feet (100 m) underwater to study marine life.

Protecting the environment

Cousteau knew that his international fame as an underwater explorer and filmmaker could help environmental groups. Over the next 35 years, he supported many causes that campaigned to protect the environment and animal and marine life. In particular, he has campaigned for the **conservation** of the seabed, and to protect the environment of Antarctica.

Tests in the Pacific

In 1995 Cousteau protested to the French government about their plans to test nuclear bombs in the Pacific Ocean. The tests were still conducted, but the French authorities have decided, due to pressure from governments all over the world, that there will be no more tests.

Fighting on

At an age when most people are content to retire, Jacques Cousteau is still fighting and campaigning on behalf of environmental causes. His long life as an explorer, inventor, filmmaker, and campaigner has shown the world how fascinating and wonderful life is in the depths of the ocean. He has also proven we need to work hard to protect it.

Jacques Cousteau addressing crowds at a New York City rally against nuclear tests in the Pacific Ocean.

NELSON MANDELA

Born 1918

For over fifty years, Nelson Mandela campaigned for the abolition of apartheid in South Africa. He spent 27 years in prison. Four years after his release, in 1990, he was elected president of South Africa.

White people began to move to South Africa in the seventeenth century. The first settlers were Dutch, and they were followed by people from France and Great Britain. The native South Africans lived off the land, but the Europeans took the land from them and claimed it as their own.

In time, the Europeans formed a government that took control of a country where most people were black. Many white people, especially those of Dutch descent who were called Afrikaners, believed that black people were inferior.

System of apartheid

The Afrikaners insisted on **racial** separation. They believed that black and white people should live separate lives. In 1948 they established the policy of *apartheid*, which means "separation." Apartheid denied black people the right to have a say in how their country was governed or in where they lived.

Nelson Mandela's fight to end apartheid was one of the greatest political campaigns this century.

The townships

White people lived in cities, while black people lived in **townships**, or in the homelands, which were country areas set aside for black South Africans by the government. The townships were overcrowded, and the Africans who lived there lost their South African **citizenship**.

Black law firm

Nelson Mandela was born in Transkei, South Africa, in 1918. He was the son of the chief of the Tembu tribe. Nelson was sent away to school when he was nine years old. He worked hard and went on to study law. He finished law school in 1942, and went to live in Johannesburg, where he set up the first black law firm in South Africa. Mandela tried to help black people by representing them in court and fighting for their rights.

The ANC

The African National Congress (ANC) was established in 1912. Its aim was to bring together all Africans in their fight for equal rights. In 1925 the ANC adopted a flag of black (for the people), green (for the land), and gold (for the resources). For the next 35 years, the ANC campaigned for **democracy** in South Africa, but in 1960 ANC was banned by the government as an unlawful organization.

Because of apartheid, there were separate restrooms for black and white people.

Joining the ANC

In 1944 Mandela joined the African National Congress and became one of its leaders. He organized protests against the government and led peaceful demonstrations against segregation. The government responded by attacking protesters and arresting thousands of ANC supporters, but the demonstrations continued throughout the 1950s.

Spear of the Nation

In 1960 thousands of Africans gathered for an anti-apartheid demonstration in Sharpeville. The Africans were unarmed, but the police opened fire on them, and 69 people were shot dead. The government banned the ANC, and Mandela realized that the days of peaceful protest were over.

After much discussion the ANC decided to form a **guerrilla** army called Umkhonto we Sizwe (Spear of the Nation). This organization wanted to overthrow the white government. They began planning acts of **sabotage** and carrying out attacks on power plants and military and government buildings, especially those connected with the policy of apartheid.

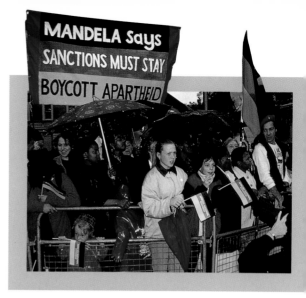

Life imprisonment

Mandela was actively involved in Umkhonto we Sizwe, and in 1962 he was arrested and sentenced to five years in prison. But the government wanted to keep him in prison for life. Their chance came in 1963, when police raided a house in the suburb of Rivonia, in Johannesburg, and found guns and equipment that belonged to Umkhonto we Sizwe.

The courtyard at Robben Island.
Nelson Mandela is one of the prisoners
sewing prison clothes in the line on the right.

Boycott

Nelson Mandela's dedication to the campaign to end apartheid inspired people all over the world to support the cause. The South African economy suffered as other countries boycotted South African goods. South Africa was expelled from the 1964 Olympic Games, and artists and entertainers refused to visit the country.

President of South Africa

In 1993 Mandela and de Klerk won the Nobel Peace Prize for their efforts to end apartheid peacefully. Mandela went on to lead the ANC in talks with the white government, which resulted in the first democratic elections ever held in South Africa. The ANC won easily and, in 1994, Nelson Mandela became the first president of the new, multiracial South Africa.

Anti-apartheid movement

The imprisoned Mandela was charged with plotting to overthrow the government, and he was sentenced to life imprisonment. He spent the next 27 years in prison, many of them under harsh conditions at Robben Island, a barren wasteland off the coast of Cape Town. But even here Mandela spoke out against the injustice of apartheid. He had huge support from the people of South Africa and from people all over the world.

Freedom at last

From 1980 on, international pressure to end racial discrimination increased. Finally, in 1990, the government lifted its ban on the ANC. On February 11 that year, the government leader, President F. W. de Klerk, released Nelson Mandela from prison.

   All over the world, millions of people switched on their television sets and watched the 71-year-old Nelson Mandela walk out of prison.

President Mandela addresses an international conference in Johannesburg, in 1993.

MARTIN LUTHER KING, JR.

1929–1968

Martin Luther King, Jr. was one of the greatest civil rights campaigners in history. He dedicated his life to the fight for equal rights for African Americans.

Slavery was abolished in the United States at the end of the Civil War, in 1865. But for most black people, the struggle for freedom was just beginning. Over the next hundred years, laws were passed in the southern states that deprived black people of their civil rights. They were not allowed to vote, own property, or use the same toilets, or sit in the same sections of parks, movie theaters, libraries, or restaurants as white people.

Baptist minister

Martin Luther King, Jr. was born in 1929, in Georgia, one of the southern states. When he was 15, King went to college in Atlanta, through a program for gifted students. He wanted to be a **Baptist** minister, like his father and grandfather. He earned his degree in **divinity** in 1948, and then went to Boston University, where he studied for a **doctorate**. It was there that he read about the Indian leader, Mahatma Gandhi, who had changed conditions for Indian people without using violence.

Civil rights activist Martin Luther King, Jr. Under his leadership, the Civil Rights Movement ended segregation in the southern states of America.

Rosa Parks sitting in the front of
a city bus in Alabama, in 1955.

Southern racism

While he was in Boston, King met a music
student named Coretta Scott. They married
in 1953 and went to live in the South.
They both knew how difficult life was for
black people in the South, but for them it
was home. King accepted a position as
pastor of a Baptist church in Montgomery,
Alabama – one of the most **racist** states in
America.

Civil rights

When Martin Luther King, Jr. talked about civil
rights, he was referring to the right to own
property, the right to speak freely, the right not
to be imprisoned without being charged with
an offense, and the right to be treated fairly.

In May 1953 police in Alabama sic
their dogs on civil rights protesters.

Bus boycott

King had been in Alabama for about
a year when African Americans
organized a protest against segregation
on public buses. A black woman
named Rosa Parks sat in a seat that
was reserved for white people and
refused to move. She was arrested,
because in Alabama, black people
were forced to sit in the backs of the
buses. People were outraged by her
arrest and boycotted the bus
company. King became involved in
the boycott, and he was later chosen
by the protesters to be their leader.

Victorious outcome

African Americans in Alabama were
prepared to walk long distances rather than
travel on the buses. They demanded that the
bus company let them sit where they wanted.
The bus company held out for a year, but it
lost so much money that it was forced to give
in to the protesters. The campaigners were
triumphant, and the Civil Rights Movement
had made an important victory.

Nobel Prize Winner

The Nobel Prize was named after Alfred Bernhard Nobel, a Swedish chemist who invented dynamite. When he died, Nobel stated in his will that his fortune should go toward setting up a system of awards that would be given every year to people who made great contributions in the fields of physics, chemistry, medicine, literature, and world peace. The Nobel Peace Prize was first awarded in 1901. Since then some of the most famous people this century have won the award. Martin Luther King, Jr. won it in 1964. In 1993 Nelson Mandela and F. W. de Klerk won it jointly for peacefully ending apartheid in South Africa.

Nonviolent protest

In 1957 King helped start the Southern Christian Leaders Conference (SCLC), which brought together all the civil rights groups. He traveled all over the country, giving lectures to tell his followers that the best way for African Americans to win equal rights was to protest in nonviolent ways.

For whites only

In 1960 King agreed to support sit-ins by blacks in whites-only restaurants in Georgia and Alabama. When black protesters entered the restaurants, they were attacked by angry white people. The events were shown on television, and people all over America saw how the nonviolent black protesters were treated. King was arrested and sentenced to four months of hard labor. But there was a massive public outcry, and, with the help of the President of the United States at the time, John F. Kennedy, King was released.

People pouring sugar, ketchup, and mustard over a black girl and her white friends in a whites-only restaurant in Jackson, Mississippi.

I Have a Dream...

In August 1963, King organized a march in Washington, D. C., to demand equal justice for all people. Over 250,000 people marched with him and heard him give his famous "I Have a Dream" speech. In this speech, King spoke of a society where racism and discrimination did not exist. The following is an excerpt:

I have a dream that one day on the red hills of Georgia the sons of former slaves and the sons of former slaveowners will be able to sit down together at the table of brotherhood.

I have a dream that my four little children will one day live in a nation where they will not be judged by the color of their skin but by the content of their character.

Martin Luther King, Jr. speaks to the crowd at the March on Washington, in 1963.

Civil Rights Act of 1964

The following year, the United States Congress passed the most important Civil Rights Act yet, which made segregation and discrimination in public places illegal. Also in 1964, Martin Luther King, Jr. was awarded the Nobel Peace Prize for fighting injustice without using violence.

The promised land

King continued to campaign, turning his attention to solving problems such as poverty and unemployment. In April 1968, he went to Memphis, Tennessee. In his speech on April 3, he told his followers, "I may not get to the promised land with you, but I want you to know tonight that we as a people will." The next day he was shot dead. Martin Luther King, Jr. had fought all his life for equal rights for African Americans. He achieved so much without even once using violence.

GLOSSARY

Abolition   Putting an end to something.

Armory   A place where weapons and military equipment are kept.

Assassinate   To murder a person by a surprise attack.

Baptist   A member of the Protestant denomination that practices baptism by immersion.

Boycott   To refuse to have anything to do with a person or organization.

Caulking   Making the bottom of a boat or ship watertight by filling in the cracks between the planks.

Citizenship   The right to be a member of a country and to live there.

Civil disobedience   Breaking the law without using violence.

Civil rights   The rights of everyone to live and speak freely, to own property, and to be treated fairly.

Colonies   Land settled and governed by people from another part of the world.

Congress   A group of people who make the laws of a country.

Conservation   The protection of the environment.

Cruise missiles   Small, low-flying weapons with nuclear warheads.

Democracy   A country ruled by a government chosen by the people who live there.

Deport   To force someone to leave a country.

Discrimination   Unfair treatment of a person because of his or her race, color, religion, or sex.

Divinity   The study of God.

Doctorate   A degree of a doctor of philosophy. It is the highest degree of learning one can earn.

Emigrate   To leave one country to live in another.

Excise   Taxes on goods such as alcohol.

Extremist   A person with very strong political ideas.

Fraud   Cheating or lying to gain money.

French Resistance   A secret organization that fought against the Nazi occupation of France in World War II.

Guerrilla   A fighter who wages war by ambush and surprise attack.

Illiteracy   Being unable to read and write.

Insurrection   A rebellion against a government.

Martyr   Someone who suffers or dies for their beliefs.

Militant   Willing to fight.

Munitions   Military stores and equipment.

Nationalist   Someone who wants their country to be free of foreign rule.

Noncooperation   Refusing to work with other people or countries as a protest against them.

Oceanographic   Having to do with the study of the ocean.

Pacifist   One who is opposed to war.

Partition   To divide a country into separate areas.

Pastor   A clergyperson.

Penal colonies   Prisons in foreign countries where convicts were sent.

Pension   A gratuity granted as a favor or reward.

Prow   The front of a ship or boat.

Racial   Having to do with race.

Racial harassment   Treating people badly because of their race.

Racist   Believing that people of some races are better than others.

Radical   An extreme political view.

Radioactive   Something that gives off harmful nuclear rays.

Reactor   A container in which chemical reactions produce nuclear energy.

Regiments   Military units.

Republic   A state governed by the people or their elected representatives.

Sabotage   To destroy or disrupt.

Segregation   Forcing people of different races to live apart.

Shield   A strong barrier around a nuclear reactor that keeps dangerous radioactive rays from escaping.

Shrine   A place that is important to a religion or connected with a famous person or event.

Tannery   A place where animal hides and skins are made into leather.

Townships   Depressed South African towns where black Africans were forced to live before the end of apartheid.

Toxic waste   Poisonous chemicals that can damage or kill plants and animals.

Treason   The crime of betraying one's country, usually by trying to overthrow the government.

Women's suffrage   The right for women to vote.

INDEX